SPACE STATION MARS

BILLY	NEIL	BOBBY
PILOT	SCIENTIST	COMMANDER
CRAIG	GYROTRON	MIKE
NAVIGATOR	ALIEN	TREASURER
ANDY	DANNY	MOLLY
ASTRONAUT	SPACE CADET	SPACE DOG

Daniel San Souci

A Clubhouse Book

TRICYCLE PRESS
Berkeley / Toronto

For my daughters Yvette and Noelle,
and my son Justin.

The publisher wishes to thank Bob Logsdon for his photograph of the crystal radio set provided from the wireless collection of Randall Renne and used with the owner's kind permission.

Photograph of the Valley View Reservoir is used with the kind permission of East Bay Municipal Utility District.

Tricycle Press
a little division of Ten Speed Press
P.O. Box 7123
Berkeley, California 94707
www.tenspeed.com

Design by Tasha Hall based on a previous design by Toni Tajima and Daniel San Souci
Typeset in Stinky Butt

Library of Congress Cataloging-in-Publication Data

San Souci, Daniel.
    Space Station Mars / Daniel San Souci.
        p. cm. — (A Clubhouse book)
        Summary: The Dangerous Snake and Reptile club, with the help of a boy visiting the neighborhood, sets up equipment in the clubhouse in hopes of tracking flying saucers and making contact with aliens.
        ISBN 1-58246-142-2
    [1. Extraterrestrial beings—Fiction. 2. Unidentified flying objects—Fiction. 3. Clubs—Fiction.] I. Title.
        PZ7.S1946Sp 2005
        [Fic]—dc22   2004028619

First Tricycle Press printing, 2005
Printed in Singapore

1 2 3 4 5 6 – 09 08 07 06 05

Author's Note

The school children I have talked with over the years are always interested to hear that my brother Robert and I have published many children's books together. They also love listening to stories about the adventures we had growing up. We feel that our childhood was magical and is what inspired us to create books. Here is one of our favorite stories.

One summer afternoon, Billy, Craig, and Andy met me and my brothers at the clubhouse. My dad promised to drive us to the matinee in the Shipwreck.

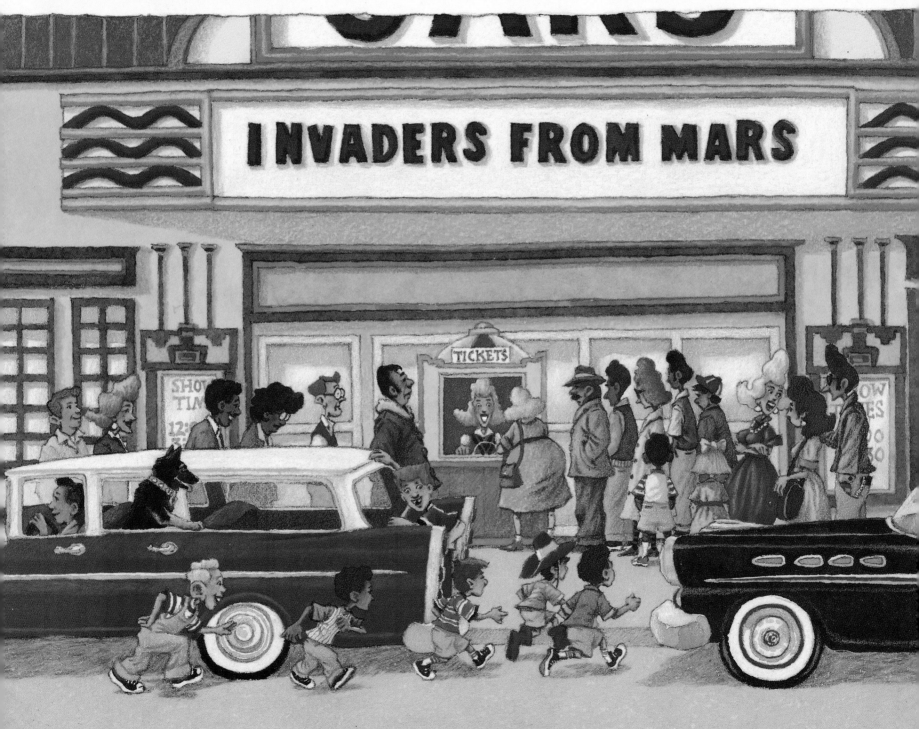

The theater was packed. The movie was really scary.

We were all glad when it was finally over, except for my older brother, Bobby. He said he wanted to see it seven more times.

That night we slept over in the clubhouse. We kept talking about the movie and went outside.

Bobby pointed out Mars. "I bet there are flying saucers above us right now from that planet," he said.

Suddenly a streak of light flashed across the sky.
"There goes one now!" yelled my younger brother, Mike.

"That's just a shooting star," said Billy. "Flying saucers don't go that fast!"

"A shooting star is a meteor that's burning up," said Andy.

"A meteor is a rock from outer space and sometimes they crash on Earth," said Bobby.

"They kind of look like regular rocks," said Craig.

I suddenly remembered something. "The other day I saw a meteor in Mrs. Gray's backyard."

In the morning I showed everyone the meteor.

"Stand back!" warned Bobby. "It might be radioactive!"

We went home and made some gear to protect us from danger. Then we carried the meteor back to the clubhouse.

Later on that day, Bobby showed up with Neil, who was spending a few weeks with his grandmother across the street.

"He's going to test the meteor for us," said Bobby.

Neil opened up his chemistry set.

"Hmm . . . very interesting," he murmured.

He did a quick experiment. There was lots of foam and it smelled awful. "Only a meteor would stink *this* bad!" he said.

Neil looked at some particles from the meteor under a microscope. "It's definitely Martian," he concluded. "Everyone take a look. You'll see why it can only be from Mars."

We took turns looking in the microscope. And we all agreed this was proof that the meteor was from Mars.

"Now the big question," Neil said.
"Is this Martian meteor radioactive?"
He ran test after test.

"Good news," he finally said. "It's not!"

"Whew," we all sighed.

Besides being a meteor expert, Neil knew lots of other things about outer space.

In his grandmother's garage we saw Neil's stuff from home. He had star charts, and maps of the universe, and books with pictures of what aliens really look like. But best of all, he had a telescope and a crystal radio he built by himself.

"As soon as I decide where to set up this equipment, I'm going to start making contact with aliens."

"You can set up in our clubhouse," offered Bobby.

"Then we can help you contact aliens," I added.

Neil nodded. "The clubhouse would be the perfect place to track flying saucers!"

The next day we renamed the

clubhouse "Space Station Mars."

In the evenings, when it got dark, we would all meet.

Neil listened to noises
from outer space on his crystal
radio. He scribbled information in
a code that only he knew.
"What we are doing is *top secret*," he said.

Mike and Andy worked the telescope. They searched the skies for flying saucers.

Bobby and Billy used colored stick pins to track flying saucers crossing the galaxy.

My job was to draw pictures of aliens for the clubhouse walls. Craig's job was to hold the flashlight, so I could see what I was doing.

The first few days all Neil picked up was odd crackling on the radio.

"It's coming from the far end of the galaxy," he said. "But it's a language I'm not familiar with!"

One evening, strange events started to unfold. Mike and Andy spotted a blinking light between the moon and Professor Stern's chimney.

There was so much static and crackling on the crystal radio that Neil warned, "Something big is about to happen."

Just then, Bobby moved a yellow stick pin. "We've got a flying saucer about to land on Earth!" he yelled.

"What do they want?" I asked.

Neil jumped out of his chair.

"I know," he said. "It's the same thing that happened in a comic book I read."

We had no idea what he was talking about.

He took the meteor from its shelf.

"The aliens want this back. It's an energy force that keeps life going on their planet."

"Ohhh . . . ," we said.

The next evening Dad asked Mom, "Have you seen that dome-shaped thing across from the park?"

"I don't recall anything like that," she replied.

"Just now, when I was driving home from work, I saw it," he said. "Funny, I never noticed it before."

"What does it look like?"

"I guess it kind of looks like . . . a flying saucer," he said. "What's for dinner?"

The second Bobby and I heard what Dad said, we raced to the phone to call an emergency meeting at Space Station Mars.

We decided we had to give the meteor back to the aliens. "Aliens are unpredictable," warned Neil. "If we see any, I will make contact and return their meteor."

We all agreed that he was best for the job.

We started on our journey first thing in the morning.

It didn't take long to find the flying saucer.

By taking a few shortcuts we made it in good time.

It was bigger than we could have ever imagined.

Then something amazing happened. Two aliens with ray guns came out of nowhere!

Neil picked up the meteor and started walking towards them.

"I hope they don't shoot their ray guns," I said to Bobby.

"If they do, I'm cutting out of here!" he replied.

Neil stood right in front of the aliens. I was so nervous that my knees shook.

He handed the meteor to one of them and said, "Here is what you have come to Earth to find."

Neil turned and slowly walked back to where we were hiding.

"Ditch!" shouted Bobby, and we raced away.

"Hey, why did that kid hand you that rock?" asked one of the painters.

"I have no idea," the other said. "But we better get to work. We still have the entire back side of this water tank to paint."

Oak Hills
Water Tank

On the news that night, we heard that an unexplained electrical surge knocked out the power to the city for a short time. We figured it was caused by the flying saucer taking off for Mars.

A few days later Neil's parents showed up, loaded his stuff in the trunk of their car, and drove him home.

A week before school was to start, we received a letter from Neil.

But we couldn't read it because it was in secret code.

Crystal Radio Set

When I was a youngster, many kids sent away for a kit to build a crystal radio set out of a round Quaker Oats box. The kit only had a few parts and could be assembled in a short time.

When completed, it picked up radio waves without needing any batteries or electrical power. At that time crystal radios were very popular with amateur radio enthusiasts. They were also popular with schoolchildren and scouts because building them taught basic electronics.

If you want to find out about some fourth graders who made their own crystal radios, check out www.tompolk.com/crystalradios/cedarcreek.html.

Alien Ship or Curious Structure?

This water tank, called the Valley View Reservoir, is located in the hills to the east of San Francisco Bay. You can see why we thought it was a flying saucer that had landed!

Decode Neil's Secret Message

⊙ ≈ A   ⊌ ≈ E   ⊌ ≈ I   ✛ ≈ M   ≈≈ ≈ Q   ▣ ≈ U   ≈ Y

][≈ B   ⍲ ≈ F   ⋈ ≈ J   ⊍ ≈ N   ⊟ ≈ R   ⚲ ≈ V   ⊔ ≈ Z

ⵣ ≈ C   ☾ ≈ G   ⌗ ≈ K   ☰ ≈ O   ⚵ ≈ S   ⌓ ≈ W

⚲ ≈ D   ⤢ ≈ H   ¢ ≈ L   ⚏ ≈ P   ⊅ ≈ T   ⧊ ≈ X

Log on to www.tricyclepress.com/clubhousebooks for the solution and look for more Clubhouse adventures in *The Amazing Ghost Detectives* and *The Dangerous Snake and Reptile Club*.